Library of Congress Control Number 2008909241

Published by Mullins Publications, LLC

Printed in the United States of America.

First Edition

ISBN: 0-9760160-0-1

ISBN 13: 9780976016007

To order additional copies visit www.booksurge.com,
www.amazon.com or call 1-866-308-6235.

www.angelfingersfoundation.org

Dedicated to the angel of my life

Na'Dya Trufant

With love, dad

Bobby Trufant

ANGEL FINGERS SERIES

Na'Dya Goes to School

by Bobby & Tia Trufant

Mullins Publications, LLC

Na'Dya's dad explains to her teacher, Ms. Mullins, her physical challenge.

"Good morning class. Please welcome our new student Na'Dya. Notice that Na'Dya's hands are different from ours, but keep in mind that we are all different in our own way. Let's take a moment to recognize the differences in each of us."

Na'Dya is told to sit at the purple table.
The recess bell rings.

Su Lin notices Na'Dya standing alone.

Na'Dya wants to play, but Selena notices that Na'Dya does not have enough fingers. Na'Dya sadly walks away.

"My name is Su Lin. I'll be your friend."

Su Lin comforts her new friend Na'Dya.

Na'Dya and Su Lin play patty cake. Recess is over.

"Tomorrow is show and tell. Please bring something special to share with us."

Na'Dya tells her dad that Selena was mean to her. Dad says, "It's okay honey, she just doesn't understand."

In her dream, Na'Dya's guardian angel appears.

The angel says, "Don't be sad my child. God has given you many gifts."

Na'Dya's guardian angel spreads her wings and Na'Dya notices that their fingers are just alike.

Na'Dya says, "Wow! I have angel fingers!"

29

The next day Na'Dya amazes the class as she plays "Mary Had A Little Lamb" on her violin.

Ms. Mullins says, "Na'Dya, I'm so proud of you!"

Su Lin is so proud of Na'Dya that she gives her a big hug.

THE END

Made in the USA